For Archie and Tilly, who bravely eat eggplant parmigiana (sometimes) – AL

For Michael, I love you. Thank you for putting up with me – KK

PUFFIN BOOKS

UK | USA | Canada | Ireland | Australia
India | New Zealand | South Africa | China

Penguin
Random House
Australia

Penguin Random House Australia is part of the Penguin Random House group of companies whose addresses can be found at global.penguinrandomhouse.com.

First published by Puffin Books, an imprint of Penguin Random House Australia Pty Ltd, in 2021

Cover design by Rebecca King © Penguin Random House Australia Pty Ltd
Typeset in 16/24 pt Adobe Garamond by Midland Typesetters, Australia
Author photo © Daniel Boud

Printed and bound in China

A catalogue record for this book is available from the National Library of Australia

NATIONAL LIBRARY OF AUSTRALIA

ISBN 978 1 76104229 4 (Paperback)

Penguin Random House Australia uses papers that are natural and recyclable products, made from wood grown in sustainable forests. The logging and manufacture processes are expected to conform to the environmental regulations of the country of origin.

penguin.com.au

Andrew Levins

NELSON
Eggplants
and
Dinosaurs

Illustrated by
Katie Kear

PUFFIN BOOKS

Chapter 1

Nelson Hunter hated vegetables. He hated looking at them, he hated smelling them. But most of all, he hated carrying them in a bumbag around his waist.

You see, eating vegetables gave Nelson superpowers. Pumpkin made him super strong. Broccoli turned him invisible. His weird grandma told him

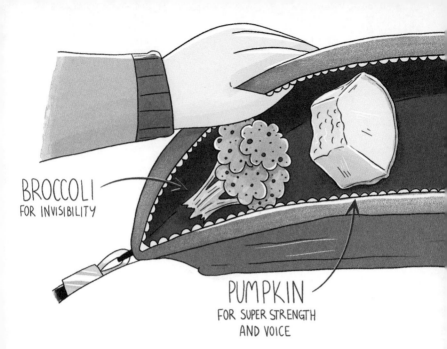

BROCCOLI
FOR INVISIBILITY

PUMPKIN
FOR SUPER STRENGTH
AND VOICE

that other vegetables would give him
other superpowers too, but Nelson had
no desire to find out. It was bad enough
that he was now regularly forcing himself
to eat pumpkin and broccoli.

Nelson was using his superpowers to
be a superhero. And he wasn't that bad

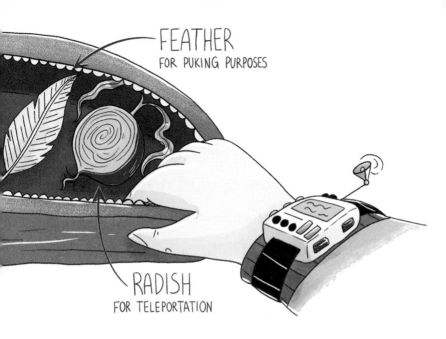

FEATHER
FOR PUKING PURPOSES

RADISH
FOR TELEPORTATION

at it. In the past couple of weeks he'd stopped an alien from eating his teacher, escaped a secret government base inside a volcano and, right now, he was about to use his superpowers for the most noble deed of all: rescuing a cat that was stuck up a tree.

Nelson had barely slept the night before because of the cat's loud meowing coming from the tree outside his window. It wasn't until that afternoon that he'd realised where the meowing was coming from: his neighbour's cat Misty, stuck in the frangipani tree. Misty had obviously climbed up the highest branch and had no idea how to get down.

'Look at the time,' said Nelson to himself as he looked up at the helpless Misty. 'It's hero-o'clock.'

It was actually 3.30 pm.

Up Nelson climbed, branch after branch. He didn't even need to use his superpowers for this one. That meant he wouldn't need to eat any gross veggies.

'Here, kitty,' said Nelson to the spooked cat. 'Let's get you home.'

Nelson reached out to Misty a little too quickly. Misty hissed and swiped at his hand.

'Ow!' shouted Nelson, forgetting he was in a tree. He let go of the branch so he could rub his scratched hand, but then scratched himself even more when he fell out of the tree, banging every branch on the way down and landing hard on the ground. Nelson patted his sore butt as the pink and yellow flowers

of the shaken tree rained down around him.

Maybe this cat didn't need saving after all. Nelson was just about to go back inside when he realised: if he didn't get Misty out of the tree now, she'd be up meowing all night again, and he'd wake up tomorrow even grouchier than the cat. He needed to sneak up on her. Luckily, this is where his superpowers came in handy.

Nelson had started to keep a handful of vegetables, the sickening source of his superpowers, in a bumbag around his waist. Nelson didn't like being so close to the things he hated most in the universe, but having them on him made his superpowers a lot easier to access than trying to find a pumpkin every time he needed to be strong enough to lift a car above his head. He unzipped his bumbag and pulled a piece of broccoli out. It was slightly squished (the bumbag had broken Nelson's fall from the tree) and was starting to stink after being in the bag for a few days.

'I'm doing this for you, Misty,' whispered Nelson, heroically. He stuffed the squished, stinky broccoli into his mouth and forced himself to chew as quickly as possible. Nelson swallowed with a gulp, instantly turned invisible and made his way back up the frangipani tree.

This time, he was able to get right up next to Misty without her noticing. He reached one hand around the grumpy cat and tried to pull her from the branch. Misty didn't budge. Nelson tried to pull her again. No luck. She dug her claws into the branch as deep as possible and started to hiss through her teeth.

Nelson was going to need a little assistance. He let go of Misty and unzipped his bumbag again, this time pulling out a piece of pumpkin. 'Okay, I lied,' said Nelson to himself as he lifted the soggy piece of pumpkin to his mouth. 'I'm not doing this for Misty, I'm doing this for myself. All I want is a good night's sleep. Is that too much to ask?!'

Nelson shoved the pumpkin down his throat and was immediately ten times stronger. He ripped Misty away from the branch and jumped out of the tree with her in his arms. The ground shook as they landed. He slowly lowered

the spooked cat to the ground and she
bolted back to her house.

Nelson breathed a sigh of relief.
Another heroic adventure completed!
Time to call it a day.

Suddenly, Nelson's watch beeped loudly with the unmistakable sound of an emergency distress signal. His day was far from over.

Chapter 2

'Broccoli Boy, do you copy?' said a voice coming from Nelson's watch. The voice belonged to Olive Sadana – Nelson's best friend and one of four people who knew about Nelson's superpowers. Nelson could hear her but, because he'd eaten broccoli, he was invisible – and so was his watch. The only way for Nelson to turn his superpowers off was to either wait a few hours for them to wear off, or to expel the vegetables from his body by making himself throw up.

'Broccoli Boy, are you there?' asked Olive. 'Pumpkin Pal, do you read me?'

While Olive called him names, Nelson reached into his bumbag and pulled out a cockatoo feather. The feather was long and white with a yellow tip. Nelson opened his mouth and stuck the feather right down the back of his throat and started tickling his tonsils.

BLEUGH!

Nelson vomited pieces of chewed-up pumpkin and broccoli onto the ground beneath him (thankfully missing his shoes – his aim got better with each spew), wiped his mouth and looked at his now-visible spy watch.

'Ah, there you are,' laughed Olive. 'The one and only Captain Vomit.'

'I told you to stop calling me that!' yelled Nelson into his watch. The watches were given to Nelson and Olive by his grandma, who used to be a spy. She knew about Nelson's superpowers as well. So did Nelson's teacher, Mr Shue (the one who Nelson had saved from being eaten by an alien), and a super-cool spy named Agent Cherry, who Nelson had met inside a volcano.

'And *I* told *you* we need superhero names!' said Olive. 'So what do you want me to call you?'

Nelson groaned as his friend laughed way too loud at her own joke.

'*Please*, just call me Nelson,' begged Nelson, wiping his lips on his sleeve. 'And, please, tell me what the emergency is!'

'The emergency, Nelson,' said Olive, 'is that we need you to stop the school library from being robbed.'

Nelson scrunched his face up in disgust. His last adventure had taken him inside a volcano, and now Olive wanted him to go on an adventure to his school on a *Sunday*?

'Why would anyone want to steal from the school library?' yawned Nelson. 'I've done enough heroic stuff today. I'm going for a nap.'

'I insist you help us, Nelson,' boomed another, older voice from Nelson's watch. The voice belonged to Agent Cherry, the coolest secret agent Nelson had ever met (and he'd met at least five so far). Her tiny face appeared next to Olive's tiny face on Nelson's tiny watch screen.

'Over the past week, someone has been stealing every book about dinosaurs from every library and bookshop in the

country,' said Agent Cherry. 'I'm talking every dinosaur encyclopedia, every palaeobiology almanac, every prehistoric comic book – gone. Right now, the only book left about dinosaurs is a copy of *My First Dinosaur ABCs*, and it just happens to be inside your school library. We need you to get in there and protect that dinosaur alphabet book with your life!'

Nelson took a deep breath and closed his eyes. He knew all about that book. *My First Dinosaur ABCs* was the only book he'd borrowed in kindergarten. It had taught him the ABCs, from *Allosaurus* to *Zuniceratops*, and he wasn't going to let this important piece of literature disappear. Even if it meant breaking into his school library on a Sunday afternoon.

'Fine, if nobody else can do it, I'll go to school and save the book,' sighed Nelson into his watch. 'But someone's going to have to lend me money for the bus.'

Chapter 3

Nelson stood outside the front gate of his school as the sun started to set. He had broken in once before. A year ago, Mr Shue had discovered a comic book that Nelson was hiding inside his maths book. Just before Nelson was about to find out the identity of the villain, Mr Shue had taken the comic and locked it in his desk drawer. He'd said Nelson could have it back the next day, but Nelson couldn't wait that long! That night, he'd jumped over the school fence, but the school's alarm had gone off so Nelson had climbed back over and sprinted all the way home.

This time was different though. The school alarm wouldn't be able to detect Nelson if he was invisible. His fingers returned to the bumbag that was clipped around his waist and reached inside. Avoiding the pumpkin and radish (he didn't need those yet), Nelson grabbed a slimy piece of steamed broccoli and felt a shiver run down his spine as he touched it. He lifted the broccoli to his mouth and pinched his nose to stop the foul green stench from wafting into his nostrils. He couldn't believe he had to eat broccoli twice in one day, but he was a hero now and sometimes heroes had to make difficult choices in order to save lives – or dinosaur-themed alphabet books.

Nelson closed his eyes and counted down from five.

'Five, four, three, two . . .'

Nelson paused for a moment, then shouted the final number.

'ONE!'

Chomp. Nelson swallowed the broccoli in one bite and turned invisible.

Superpowers are awesome, he thought as he jumped over the fence and heard nothing but silence when he landed. Nelson looked over at the school's security camera and saw ... that it had been dismantled! Wires hung loosely from the roof, and the usually red blinking light was neither

red nor blinking. He wondered if the caretaker was doing some alarm-system maintenance.

Nelson saw a blue light shining from inside the school library. He wondered who was inside. A shiver ran down Nelson's spine as he considered that the book thief could already be inside his school!

The door to the library was wide open. Nelson snuck through it and crept past the non-fiction books, towards the blue light. He could hear noises coming from the Young Readers section. As he got closer, Nelson saw someone searching through the bookshelves. The someone was shiny and silver. They looked like they were made of metal, with bright blue lights for eyes. Was there a robot in Nelson's library?

Nelson could hear the robot muttering. '*My First Atlas, My First Ballet, My First Dot-to-Dot.*' It flicked through the books on the shelf. 'Where is *My First Dinosaur ABCs*?'

Nelson knew exactly where that book was. The librarian kept it in the section of books that weren't allowed to be borrowed after a certain kindergarten student didn't return it for an entire year. Nelson tiptoed over to the section, grabbed the book and quietly made his way back to the door.

The robot stopped flicking through books, noticing a dinosaur alphabet book floating through the air.

Oops! Nelson was invisible, but the book he was holding wasn't.

The robot raised its hand and fired a laser towards Nelson. Nelson jumped

out of the way and the laser blew a *Where's Wally?* book to smithereens instead. Nelson quickly tossed the dinosaur book out the door, hoping the robot would follow the book outside so he could attack from behind.

'I may not be able to see you,' said the robot, 'but my heat sensors can!'

The robot grabbed Nelson and thrust him up into the air. The robot's arms extended so that Nelson was pressed up against the ceiling. It was strong, but Nelson knew he could make himself stronger. He wrestled one arm free, unzipped his bumbag and grabbed a mushy chunk of pumpkin from his pouch of horrors. He didn't have time to count down this time. He simply closed his eyes and stuffed the disgusting pumpkin down his throat.

The effect was instant. Nelson was now invisible AND super strong. He pushed himself down from the ceiling, pulled the robotic hand from around his waist and squeezed the robot's arm until it started to spark. The robot screamed and aimed its other laser at Nelson. Nelson quickly kicked it away, causing the robot to shoot itself in the head. There was a bright flash of light and the robot's head went flying across the room, crashing into a shelf of graphic novels. The robot's body fell to the floor, sparking and smouldering as Nelson made his way over to the head. He picked up the shiny metal head and peered inside. It was empty! This wasn't a head at all – it was a helmet!

Nelson looked back at the robot's body to see it climbing back up onto its feet. And where the head used to be was now a smaller, very human-like head with long blonde hair. Nelson gasped. There was a lady inside the robot suit! This whole time, Nelson thought he'd been fighting a robot, not a person. How was she so strong?

Angry, and still a little stunned, the lady in a robot suit made her way to the door, grunting with each step. Nelson climbed over a fallen bookshelf that was between him and her. Without her helmet, she could no longer use her heat vision to see Nelson, but as he approached the door, he remembered that he wasn't her target.

The robot lady stepped outside and held her still-working laser over the copy of *My First Dinosaur ABCs* that Nelson had tossed out the door before their fight.

'NOOOOO!' shouted Nelson.

Pumpkin didn't just make his muscles extra strong, it also made his voice incredibly powerful. Nelson's super-powered voice hit the robot lady just as she fired, knocking her robot body to the floor once again and slamming her into the doors to the school's canteen.

Nelson ran towards the book, frantically picking it up. It was only lightly singed. The students of Greenmore West Primary School would be able to learn that A was for *Allosaurus* and Z was for *Zuniceratops* for many more years.

The robot lady scrunched her face up and tried to fire more rounds of lasers at the book, but both her weapons were a mess of sparks and smoke now. Nelson's pumpkin powers had busted them up good.

'Fine. You win this round, whoever you are,' she said with a grin. 'But I'll be back for that book.'

She clicked her heels together.

She was wearing rocket boots! The robot lady shot up into the sky, leaving Nelson alone in his school on a Sunday afternoon clutching a lightly singed copy of *My First Dinosaur ABCs*.

Chapter 4

Nelson sat outside the school library, deep in thought and still invisible. He'd saved the book, but the robot lady had gotten away. Should he have tried to chase after her? Maybe he could've tailed her from a distance and found the location of her secret robotics laboratory (she would definitely have one of those, right?). Nelson's invisible thoughts were interrupted by his ringing spy watch. Once again, he could hear the watch but couldn't see it. As if eating vegetables twice in one day wasn't gross enough, now he had to vomit them up twice too. The taste of vegetables going into his mouth was nowhere near as bad as the taste of them coming back out.

Nelson pulled the feather from his bumbag, worked his magic and answered Olive's call.

'Nelson! How did the mission go?' asked Olive. Before he could answer her question, Olive started chuckling. 'Nelson, you've got a little vomit on your lip.'

Embarrassed, Nelson wiped his mouth and made a mental note to pack some napkins before his next mission.

'I saved the book!' announced Nelson, proudly. 'But the thief got away.'

'Who was the thief?' asked Olive. 'And why are they stealing books?'

'It's a lady in a robot suit,' blurted Nelson. 'She can fire lasers out of her

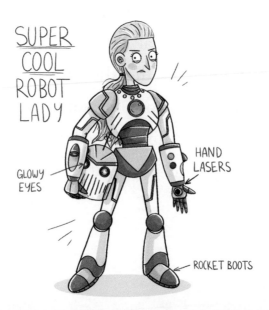

SUPER
COOL
ROBOT
LADY

GLOWY
EYES

HAND
LASERS

ROCKET BOOTS

hands. And she can fly! But I couldn't be bothered chasing after her.'

Olive smirked. Usually, she'd scold Nelson for his laziness, but this time he'd actually done the right thing.

'Your mission was to protect the book, *not* catch the thief,' Olive told Nelson. 'So mission accomplished, I guess.'

Nelson gave her the thumbs up. 'Great news,' he said. 'Now I can go to sleep.'

'I don't think so, Nelson,' said Olive. 'You're about to be late for your *next* mission.'

'Next mission?' asked Nelson, panicking. 'What do I need to do now?'

'You told my parents you'd join us for dinner tonight,' said Olive. 'And dinner will be on the table in five minutes.'

Nelson smiled. He had actually been looking forward to this dinner for weeks. He'd never eaten at the Sadanas' house before, but he'd swapped school lunches with Olive for the past four years. Her parents would always pack junk food like burger-ring sandwiches

and peanut-butter pasta. Nelson was so excited to find out what kind of delicious, nourishment-free food they would serve for dinner.

'I'll be right there,' said Nelson, reaching inside his bumbag and pulling out half a radish. Radishes allowed Nelson to teleport. Before he left for a mission, he'd slice a radish in half and take one half with him. Eating that half of the radish would then return him to where he'd left the other half.

He lifted the radish to his lips and began to count down.

'Five, four, three, two, one!'

Chomp.

Chapter 5

Nelson suddenly reappeared where the other half of the radish was: in Olive's bedroom. Olive kept half a radish near her at all times so Nelson could teleport to her whenever she needed his superpowers.

'Congratulations on a successful mission, Agent Nelson,' said Olive, taking the copy of *My First Dinosaur ABCs* from Nelson and placing it into her schoolbag for safekeeping. 'I wonder why anyone would want to steal some silly kids' book?'

'It's not silly!' said Nelson, grumpily. 'It's actually very informative and helpful for anyone who –'

Nelson stopped talking, sniffed the air and scrunched up his nose.

'What's that smell?' he asked. Olive's house did not smell like burger-ring sandwiches or peanut-butter pasta. Nelson's nostrils filled with the unmistakable stench of VEGETABLES.

Olive laughed. 'Why don't you come

to the dinner table and see?' she said, and pushed Nelson out the door.

'Nelson! I didn't even hear you come in!' said Mrs Sadana, her arms full of different-coloured dishes that she was spreading across the dining table. Nelson had no idea what any of the dishes were, but he was certain that they all contained vegetables and therefore had

to be avoided at all costs. He shuffled to the seat at the table that was furthest from the food.

'Good evening, Nelson,' said Mr Sadana as he entered the room. 'It's so nice of you to join us tonight.'

Mr Sadana placed a bowl of bright

yellow rice in front of Nelson. A quick scan showed no evidence of vegetables in the rice. Nelson grabbed the bowl and piled his plate high with rice.

'Nelson, don't just fill up on rice,' said Mrs Sadana. 'Leave some room on your plate for the curries!'

Nelson looked around the table at the many curry-filled bowls in front of them. One was bright orange, another lime green. One of the curries was purple! Nelson was overwhelmed. But Olive watched in delight.

'Would you like some palak paneer?' asked Mr Sadana, thrusting a bowl of creamy white cubes floating in a thick green sludge into Nelson's hands.

'Th-this is nothing like the food you put in Olive's lunchbox,' Nelson spluttered.

Mr Sadana smiled. 'When I was your age, my parents would stuff my lunchbox with food like this,' he said. 'Curries, rice, mango pickle, roti. They moved here from Central India, and these were the foods they would cook for me at home. But all the other children at school had sandwiches and would laugh at my lunchbox for being so different. It was very hard to fit in.'

'I wish you'd send me curry for lunch!' said Olive.

'I don't want you to get teased for it like I did,' said Mr Sadana. 'So I try my hardest to pack your lunchbox with the same junk food that all the other students eat.'

'I thought we'd be eating junk food for dinner too,' whinged Nelson. 'Like hot dogs . . . or pizza.'

Mr Sadana laughed. 'Hot dogs? Nelson, we don't even eat meat in this house.'

Nelson's heart started thumping so loudly he was sure the Sadanas could hear it.

'So does that mean that you're . . .' Nelson could barely get the words out.

'Yes, Nelson,' said Olive, proudly. 'We're vegetarians.'

HOW IT SOUNDED TO NELSON

"WE'RE VEGETARIANS!"

Nelson started to feel light headed.

'Now, can I interest you in some chana masala?' asked Mrs Sadana. 'Or some samosas? They're filled with peas.'

The *smell* of the vegetables, the *colours* of the vegetables, the *amount* of vegetables in front of Nelson was too much for him to handle. He'd already thrown up twice today and he probably wouldn't need a feather to do it again.

'Would you mind if I finished this delicious dinner outside?' he asked. 'I need some fresh air.'

Chapter 6

Nelson sat on a swing in Olive's backyard, swinging slowly and trying to forget everything he'd just seen, heard and smelled.

Olive crept outside to check up on him. 'Are you okay, Nelson?' she asked.

'I'm getting there,' replied Nelson with his eyes closed. 'This was not the meal I was expecting to eat tonight.'

'The dishes on the table are why I love vegetables so much,' said Olive. 'But I can understand how seeing that many vegetables at once might have been a little terrifying for you.'

'I'll be okay,' said Nelson. 'At least I didn't have to eat any.'

'About that . . .' said Olive. 'We can't let you leave here with an empty stomach.'

Nelson opened his eyes and saw Olive was holding a small bowl.

'What's in there?' asked Nelson, beginning to panic again.

'In here?' replied Olive. 'This is my favourite curry of all time. I've eaten it almost every day since I was a baby. It's called baingan bharta.'

Nelson started to feel dizzy. 'And what is in baingan bharta?' he asked.

'Oh, you know, a little garlic, ginger, onion,' said Olive, 'and a LOT of eggplant.'

'No way!' shouted a definitely panicking Nelson, staring at the curry in Olive's hands. 'It's so mushy and brown-looking!'

'But it's my favourite!' pleaded Olive. 'And aren't you curious about which superpower you'll get from eating eggplant?'

'Nope!' said Nelson, sharply. 'I have super strength, I can turn invisible, I can teleport. That's all I need!'

'What if eggplant can make you fly?' asked Olive, inching towards Nelson with a spoon of the eggplant curry. 'You could've chased after that thief today, no problem.'

'I guess that would come in handy,' said Nelson, his eyes fixed on the spoon slowly making its way to his mouth.

'What are you waiting for then?' asked Olive. 'Just one bite.'

Nelson closed his eyes and the two of them started counting down together.

'Five, four, three, two, one.'

Chomp.

Chapter 7

Nelson swallowed the mouthful of slightly spicy, extremely mushy eggplant curry and waited a moment, watching Olive intently watch him.

'Nothing hap–' began Nelson, before he realised that something was DEFINITELY happening. He could feel his insides starting to stretch. He clutched at his stomach, thinking he was about to let out the world's biggest burp, but then he could feel his entire body starting to stretch. It hurt! Nelson fell to the ground and started to scream.

'Nelson! Are you okay?' Olive asked her screaming friend.

He tried to answer, 'Heck no! I'm not okay!' but was only able to grit his teeth and growl.

Nelson arched his back and tensed his muscles. His body felt like it was about to explode.

Olive bent down to put her hand on his shoulder, but his shoulder suddenly grew ten times in size. Then his other shoulder did too, followed by his legs and feet.

Nelson watched Olive get smaller and smaller. Was she shrinking? Or was he growing? He could now see over Olive's roof and realised he had grown taller than a house! Nelson gasped, his face stretching to reveal a huge mouth filled with sharp white teeth. Then his butt started to stretch as a tail sprouted out of it!

Nelson looked down at his body to see that it was purple and enormous. He tried to feel his face, but his arms weren't long enough to reach it. 'What's happening to me?' he tried to ask Olive, but all that came out was, 'ROOOOOAAAARR!!'

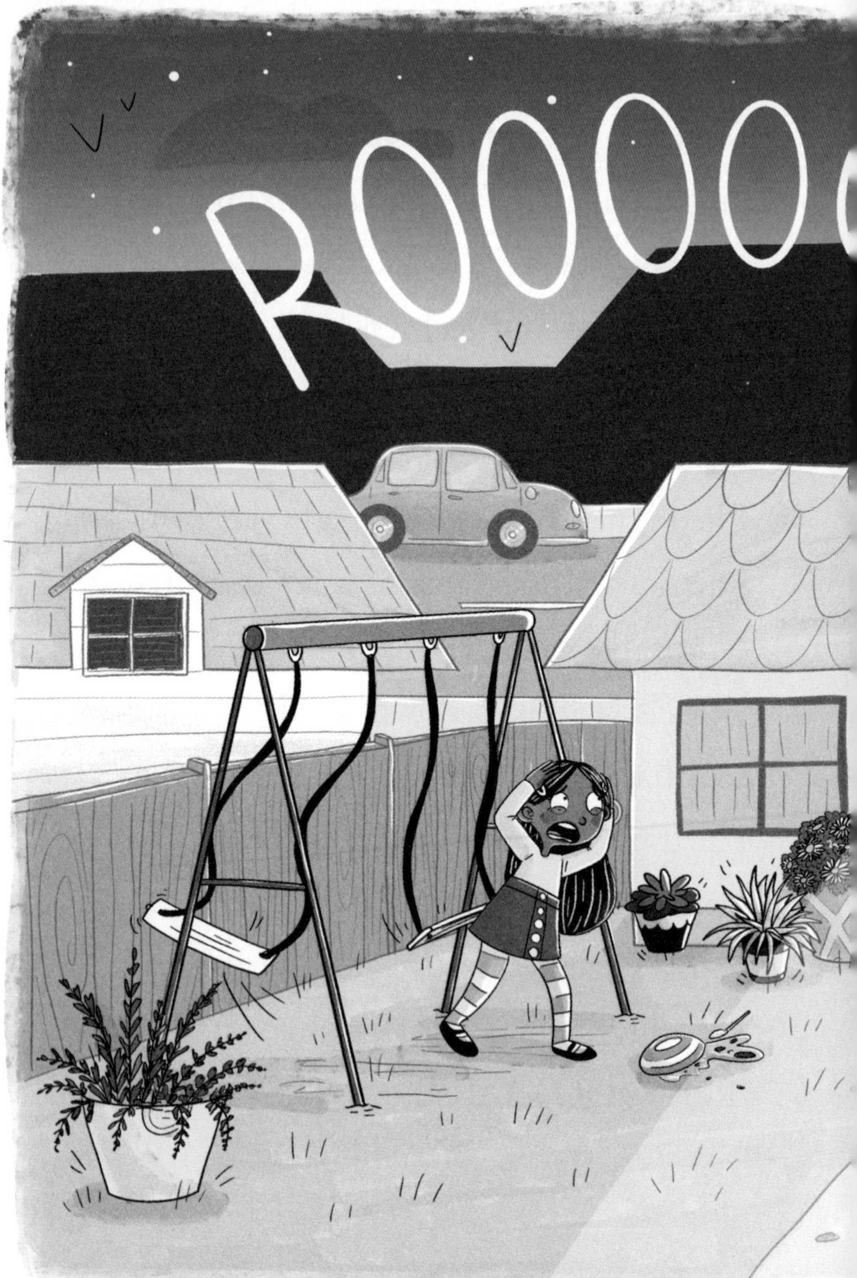
ROOOO

Nelson had turned into a dinosaur. A gigantic, purple dinosaur. With two huge feet, a long tail and a brain the size of a walnut. Nelson knew that he wasn't just any dinosaur, he had turned into the king of the dinosaurs: he was a *Tyrannosaurus rex*! Nelson stomped his big purple feet with delight, causing all the plants in Olive's backyard to shake.

Luckily, Olive's parents were listening to music like they did after every dinner, otherwise they would've heard Nelson's roars and stomps and come outside to see what was happening. Nelson's gigantic dinosaur head was peeking over the top of Olive's house though, so it wouldn't be long until someone else in the neighbourhood noticed him.

'Keep it down!' said Olive in desperation.

Nelson tried to show his excitement as quietly as possible. 'I've turned into a *T-rex*,' whispered Nelson, except all that came out was a slightly quieter 'ROOOOOOAR!'

'Stop talking!' hissed Olive. 'Someone will hear you! My parents will freak if they see a dinosaur in their backyard. You've got to make yourself throw up so you can turn back to normal.'

Easy-peasy. Nelson tried to shove his

fingers down his throat. Except his arms weren't quite long enough to reach his mouth. He tried to stretch his arm as much as possible but he lost his balance and slipped over, crushing Mr Sadana's lime tree.

Olive took a look at Nelson's sharp-teeth-filled mouth. 'There's no way I'm sticking my hand in there,' she said. 'You wait here, I'll be right back. Don't touch anything!'

Olive ran inside as Nelson tried to get back up on his massive purple feet. In the process of standing, he smashed no fewer than seven pot plants, which alerted the neighbour's dog, who jumped over the fence and started barking madly at the Nelson-saurus. Nelson turned quickly to face the dog, forgetting his long tail, which slapped the dog and sent him flying back over the fence.

Nelson turned back around and walked into an oak tree, which shook pollen into his nostrils. He sneezed so powerfully that it blew the Sadanas' fence down and sent the neighbour's dog flying once again.

'I told you not to touch anything!' said Olive, returning to her backyard with a feather duster in her hand. 'Quickly, open your mouth.'

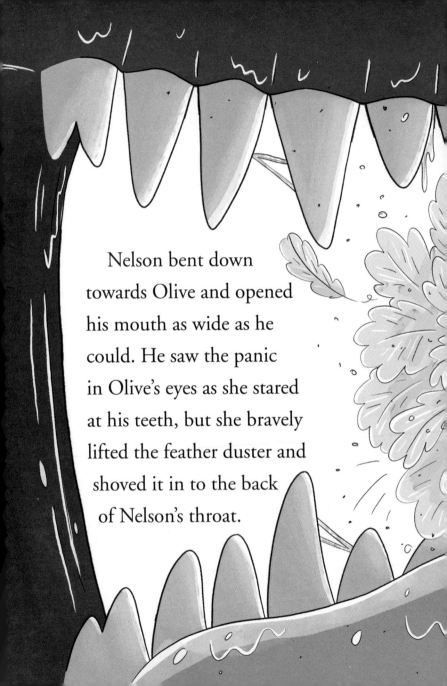

Nelson bent down
towards Olive and opened
his mouth as wide as he
could. He saw the panic
in Olive's eyes as she stared
at his teeth, but she bravely
lifted the feather duster and
shoved it in to the back
of Nelson's throat.

Nelson retched as the feather duster tickled his tonsils. He then emptied a dinosaur-sized river of eggplant vomit all over his best friend.

'Nelson,' said Olive, dripping with dino-spew, 'I think you'd better go home.'

Chapter 8

Nelson didn't eat breakfast the next morning. He was worried that his parents would ask if anything eventful happened at Olive's house the night before, so he ran out of his house as soon as he was up and dressed. He was forty-three minutes early for his bus, and he spent eleven of those minutes thinking about how much faster it would be to run to school as a dinosaur instead of taking a bus. Then he spent eight minutes thinking about how eggplants are *easily* the worst vegetables in the universe, with their dark shiny skins and slimy brown insides. Nelson spent the final twenty-four minutes thinking

about how angry Olive was going to be when she got to the bus stop too.

Olive didn't even look at Nelson as she approached the wooden seat at the bus stop. Her eyebrows sat low above her eyes, and she pursed her lips together in the biggest pout Nelson had ever seen. She was a very rare kind of angry. The kind of angry someone can only get if their best friend turns into a dinosaur and then covers them with vomit.

'I'm so, so, so, SO sorry,' said Nelson as he bravely sat down next to her.

'It's not your fault,' she sighed. 'I was the one who forced you to eat eggplant.'

'There's no way I'm ever eating eggplant again,' said Nelson.

'That better be a promise,' said Olive.

'Do you want to swap lunches?' asked Nelson. 'Mum packed me a salad sandwich.'

Olive's face dropped.

'What's wrong?' asked Nelson.

'After our talk last night, Mum and Dad decided that they'd start giving me the food I actually like to eat,' said Olive, sadly. 'And so today my lunchbox is full of baingan bharta.'

'No swapping then!' said Nelson. 'The last thing we need is me turning into a dinosaur at school. Don't be sad about it though. You told me last night that it's your favourite dish ever.'

'It *was* my favourite dish ever,' said Olive, 'until a dinosaur vomited it all over me.'

'Oh, right,' said Nelson. 'My bad.'

The two sat in awkward silence for a minute, but Nelson couldn't contain his excitement any longer.

'Vomit aside, that was pretty awesome, right?' he said to Olive. 'When I turned into a dinosaur as big as your house?'

Olive sat quietly for a moment longer.

'Vomit aside, it was pretty awesome,' she said.

'Did you see how sick my tail looked?' began Nelson.

'BUT,' she said sternly, 'if you ever, *ever* vomit on me again, I don't care how big you are, I will flatten you!'

'Loud and clear,' said Nelson. 'We'll just have to find a dinosaur-sized vomit bag for next time.'

Chapter 9

Nelson and Olive's teacher Mr Shue was late to class. His students had been sitting at their desks for almost ten minutes waiting for him to arrive when they heard his voice cheering from outside the classroom.

'Guess what, Three B?' said Mr Shue, chirpily. He entered the classroom wearing a hideous Hawaiian shirt and wheeling a suitcase. He looked happier than Nelson had ever seen him.

'What is it, Mr Shue?' asked Diana Kostopoulos from the desk next to Olive.

'I got some *tremendous* news this morning,' beamed Mr Shue. 'I won a tropical getaway vacation. All expenses paid, starting today, for the rest of the week!'

'How did you win?' asked Edwin Leota from the desk behind Nelson.

'Some teachers' association that

I didn't even know I was a member of,' said Mr Shue. 'But who cares? I won and I'm leaving today and that's all that matters, so see you later!'

'Ah, sir?' asked Olive. 'What about us?'

'Win your own holiday, Ms Sadana,' said Mr Shue. 'This one's all mine!'

'No, I mean, who will teach us this week?' asked Olive.

'Oh, right!' laughed Mr Shue. 'Allow me to introduce your teacher for the next week ...' Mr Shue beckoned towards the door.

'. . . Mrs Sock!'

A woman with gold-rimmed glasses walked in the door with a huge smile on her face. She wore a navy-blue blazer and her hair was long and blonde. Nelson thought she looked familiar, like someone he'd seen on TV or something.

'Well, that's everything, then. Have a great week, everybody,' said Mr Shue, running out the door. 'If anyone needs me, I'll be working on my tan!'

'Bye, Mr Shue,' said a confused 3B, except for Nelson, who was trying to work out where he'd seen his new teacher before. He felt like he'd seen her really recently.

'Good morning, Three B,' said Mrs

Sock, clapping her hands together. 'We're going to have quite the week together.'

Nelson recognised her voice too, but couldn't remember from where. It was a little hoarse, as if she'd been shouting a lot recently.

'I'm afraid I have a small piece of bad news,' said Mrs Sock as she walked through the classroom. 'There was a break-in at the school library over the weekend, so your library visit this afternoon has been cancelled.'

The mention of the school library triggered Nelson's memories of the night before. Nelson looked over at Mrs Sock and imagined her in a robot suit. Could it be her?

'Olive! Olive!' hissed Nelson. 'I think that's her! That's the robot lady and book thief!'

'What's this?' said Mrs Sock to Nelson, lifting her finger to her glasses. 'Rudeness in my class? Stand up, please.'

Nelson stood up.

'What's your name?' asked Mrs Sock.

Nelson started to panic. Had he said anything while they were fighting? Would she recognise his voice?

'Nelson Hunter,' he told her – with a slight British accent, just in case.

'Well, Nelson Hunter,' Mrs Sock

said. 'I don't think whispering secrets is any way to welcome a new teacher. I guess you'll have to be my first victim.'

Nelson gulped.

'Detention for you this afternoon,' she told him. 'In the library.'

'But I thought it was closed,' said Nelson.

'Oh, I'm sure they'll make a special exception for a bright student like you,' said Mrs Sock with a grin.

Nelson nodded in silence. He wondered what the thief was doing back at his school. What was she going to try to steal next?

Chapter 10

The rest of the school day was fairly uneventful. Nelson yawned his way through English, Maths and Science, resisting the urge to talk to Olive in case he got another detention. Mrs Sock was a pretty convincing teacher. Nelson kept waiting for her to crack so he could expose her for being an evil fraud, but the only evil thing she did was make the class practise their handwriting instead of letting them go to recess.

When they were finally on the playground for lunch, Nelson scraped the salad off his salad sandwich and ate the bread. Olive ate the salad. Neither of them dared open Olive's lunchbox.

'So, you think Mrs Sock is the robot lady?' asked Olive as she tucked into a piece of lettuce from Nelson's sandwich.

'I'm sure of it,' said Nelson, his mouth full of plain bread. 'I tried calling Agent Cherry during recess, but I can't get through to her. So now I have to spend detention with Mrs Sock at the scene of last night's crime.'

'Do you think she suspects that you were the one who fought her?' asked Olive.

'No idea. But if she tries anything, I'll be ready for her,' said Nelson, patting his bumbag.

'Agent Cherry mentioned she was stealing all the books about dinosaurs,' said Olive. 'So last night, after I showered and cleaned up the mess in the backyard, I tried to search for dinosaur books online. But I couldn't find anything.'

'What, they were all sold out?' asked Nelson.

'No, I mean nothing came up when I searched for *dinosaur books*,' said Olive. 'No results. Not a single mention of a book about dinosaurs anywhere. So I just searched for *dinosaur* next, then *Tyrannosaurus rex*, then any other species of dinosaur I could think of, and nothing. It's like someone's deleted every single mention of dinosaurs from the entire internet.'

'Is that even possible?' asked Nelson. Was their fake new teacher really smart enough to do that?

The bell rang as Nelson wished he was back in a volcano or fighting aliens. Those adventures made way more sense.

Chapter 11

The last lesson of the day was art class. Mrs Sock said the students could spend the afternoon drawing whatever they wanted in their art books, so Nelson took the opportunity to draw the biggest cheeseburger he'd ever seen. It was ten patties high and took up the entire page. Truly, this was

Nelson's masterpiece. He was drawing extra sauce on one of the twenty-four slices of bacon when he felt Mrs Sock breathing down his neck.

'Not bad, Nelson,' she said with a smile. 'I bet you'd be extra strong if you ate one of these every day.'

Nelson awkwardly smiled back. He wished he got his powers from eating burgers.

Mrs Sock continued making her way around the class.

'That's a beautiful rainbow,' she told Edwin. 'And I love the pencil-work on that ostrich, Diana.'

'That's supposed to be my dad,'

replied Diana. But Mrs Sock had turned her attention to something on the other side of the room.

'How dare you!' Mrs Sock shouted, stomping through the classroom. 'How dare you draw this filth in my classroom!'

Mrs Sock stood angrily above Olive's desk. Olive stopped colouring in and stared up at the teacher while holding her purple crayon in front of her face as protection.

'You said we could draw anything we wanted,' said Olive. She had drawn a gigantic purple dinosaur.

Mrs Sock gritted her teeth. 'You could've drawn anything in the entire universe,' she growled. 'And you chose to draw this pathetic creature?'

'It's just a dinosaur,' said Olive.

Just a dinosaur?!' fumed Mrs Sock. 'What is it with children and dinosaurs? Still thinking about the past when you could be drawing something from the future!'

The entire class sat in silence. This was much weirder than any of Mr Shue's rants over the years, and he once spent twenty minutes yelling about how much he hated chalk.

Mrs Sock walked to Dennis Kostopoulos's desk and made him hold up his drawing of a robot. Nelson had to stop himself from laughing. Art wasn't Dennis's best subject – it looked like a three-year-old had made his drawing.

'Now *this* is something worth drawing!' said Mrs Sock, proudly. 'So shiny, so futuristic . . . so powerful! Your little dinosaur wouldn't stand a chance against this machine marvel.'

At the desk in front of Nelson, Millie Johnson quickly flipped over her drawing of a pterodactyl. 'So are drawings of dinosaurs banned from this classroom?' Millie asked.

'They should be banned from school altogether!' said Mrs Sock, now back at Olive's desk. 'The sooner all children forget that these pitiful critters even existed, the better.'

'Does this mean our excursion to the Dinosaur Museum this Friday has been cancelled?' asked Edwin. 'I want to see their new *Stegosaurus* skeleton.'

'They've got the biggest collection of dinosaur bones in the country!' exclaimed Dennis.

'Why would I care about that?' said Mrs Sock. 'I have arranged for us to visit the Museum of Science and Technology instead.'

The entire class groaned.

'Let this be a warning to the rest of you,' shouted Mrs Sock, holding Olive's drawing above her head. 'The world is much better without dinosaurs in it!'

Rip! She tore Olive's drawing in half. The class gasped. Nelson had seen enough.

'What did you do that for?!' he blurted, standing up from his desk.

'Sit down, Mr Hunter,' said Mrs Sock. 'You've already got

detention today, but I'm open to giving you detention tomorrow too.'

Nelson sat back down.

Mrs Sock adjusted her glasses. 'And you can join Nelson in detention this afternoon, Ms Sadana,' said Mrs Sock with a scowl.

Olive finally raised her voice. 'For what?' she asked in disbelief. 'Drawing a dinosaur?!'

'Oh, don't play innocent with me,' said Mrs Sock. 'Your parents probably already know you're a terrible artist, but I bet they'll be shocked to find out that you're a thief as well.'

Olive stood up. 'I'm no thief!' she

shouted at her teacher who almost definitely *was* a thief.

'Oh, a thief and a liar then?' said Mrs Sock, placing her hands on Olive's schoolbag. 'I should have you locked up.'

'What for?' asked Olive, angrily.

'For *stealing* school property,' said Mrs Sock, reaching into Olive's schoolbag and pulling out a copy of *My First Dinosaur ABCs*. 'I know for a

fact that this book isn't allowed to leave the library. And this afternoon, you and Nelson Hunter won't be allowed to either.'

The whole class gasped again. They were used to Nelson getting detention, but this was a first for Olive.

Chapter 12

For the remaining ten minutes of school, Nelson's mind raced with a million questions. Why did Mrs Sock hate dinosaurs so much? How did she know that Olive had the book? How much trouble would Olive be in when her parents found out she'd received detention? What was going to happen during detention? Would they fight?

Why wasn't Agent Cherry returning his calls for help? Was Mr Shue actually on holiday or had he been tricked by Mrs Sock too?

The bell rang at 3 pm and everyone packed up their art supplies to go home.

'Great first day with you, Three B,' said Mrs Sock. 'I'll see most of you tomorrow morning.'

Mrs Sock looked over at Olive and Nelson. 'And I'll see you two in the library.'

Nelson and Olive walked in silence to the library. Usually, Olive would've come up with an amazing plan in a situation like this, but she was too busy thinking of what to tell her parents when they found out she'd been given detention.

When they got there, the place was empty. There weren't any seats in the library, so Nelson sat down on a beanbag. This was way comfier than the rooms he usually had detention in. Olive sat down next to him.

'How did she know I had the book?' asked Olive. 'It was like she could see inside my bag before she even opened it.'

'I swear she recognises me from our fight last night too,' said Nelson. 'She made a crack about how strong I was earlier. Plus, she gave me detention the second she saw me.'

MRS WILLIAMS   MR SMITH   MS NGUYEN

'Lots of relief teachers give you detention the second they see you, Nelson,' laughed Olive. She looked down at her watch.

'I haven't been able to get through to Agent Cherry either, by the way,' she said. 'Or your grandma.'

Nelson was about to tell Olive that maybe they should run out of there and tell the principal that something wasn't right when he heard Mrs Sock

MR WHITE

MISS KING

MR SINGH

enter the library and lock the door behind her.

'How disappointing to have to give two students detention on my first day here,' she smirked, making her way past the non-fiction section and over to where Nelson and Olive were sitting. 'There's always one rude student, but a thief as well? You're lucky I haven't called the police.'

'Play it cool, Nelson,' whispered

Olive. 'We can report her to Agent Cherry when we get home.'

Olive's warning was lost on Nelson, who immediately jumped to his feet and pointed his finger at Mrs Sock.

'Olive's not the thief, you are!' he shouted. 'You broke in and tried to steal the book last night!'

The evil grin that Nelson had seen the night before returned to Mrs Sock's face.

'Oh, you mean this book?' she said, holding up *My First Dinosaur ABCs* and placing it on the desk in front of her. 'Thank you for finding it for me.'

'How did you know it was in her

bag?' asked Nelson as he made his way towards Mrs Sock.

'You stay right where you are!' said Mrs Sock. She put her right hand in her pocket and, when she pulled it back out, it was wearing a metal glove. The same metal glove with an inbuilt laser gun that Nelson had seen yesterday. She pointed it at the book on the desk.

'If I see you take one more step, you can say goodbye to your beloved dinosaur alphabet!' she shouted.

'You won't see me do anything,' said Nelson, who had sneakily unzipped his bumbag, grabbed a piece of broccoli and shoved it in his mouth. Nelson chomped down and disappeared.

Mrs Sock squinted. 'You think you're so clever,' she said, aiming her glove directly at him. 'But I can still see you.'

'It's her glasses!' shouted Olive from behind a beanbag. 'They must be robotic with heat vision or something! That's why she can see you.'

'And X-ray vision too,' said Nelson,

climbing a bookshelf. 'That's how she was able to see the book inside your bag.'

'I can see inside that ridiculous bumbag of yours as well,' said Mrs Sock. 'So, broccoli is what makes you invisible, is it? Fascinating. I wonder what the pumpkin does?'

'Here, why don't I show you?' said Nelson, unzipping his bumbag. He was ready to fight.

'Nelson, what are you doing?' asked Olive, desperately trying to work out where Nelson was standing.

'*She* might not be able to see you, but I can,' said Mrs Sock, aiming her glove back at the book. 'Move a muscle and there's no more dinosaur alphabet.'

'Why do you hate that book so much?' asked Nelson.

'Why do children love dinosaurs so much?' said Mrs Sock. 'Ridiculous relics of the past. You kids spend every playtime pretending to stomp around like one, and then gaze in amazement at their big, dead bones in a museum.'

While Mrs Sock ranted, Nelson slowly reached into his bumbag with one finger.

'Ever since I was a child, I loved technology,' Mrs Sock continued. 'Robotics, engineering ... My peers laughed at me for my obsession with robots while they worshipped dinosaurs.

So I made a promise to myself that I would one day make a robot that was stronger than any dinosaur! Strong enough to erase the world's memory that dinosaurs ever existed in the first place.'

Nelson carefully wrapped his finger around a piece of pumpkin.

'Eliminating this final dinosaur book means I can advance to phase two of my grand plan!' shouted Mrs Sock. 'I can move on to *much* bigger targets and cause even more dinosaur destruction, and it's all thanks to you finding this book for me!'

Nelson flicked the piece of pumpkin into his mouth.

'Nice try, dino-lover,' said Mrs Sock, and she fired a laser at the book, incinerating it instantly.

Nelson watched hopelessly as burning fragments of the book floated in the air around him.

'You're going down!' said the now pumpkin-powered Nelson, his booming voice knocking books from their shelves.

Mrs Sock clicked her fingers and Nelson heard something rocketing towards him.

It was Mrs Sock's robot suit! The suit crashed into Nelson from behind, sending him flying into the wall and making books fly everywhere. Nelson quickly recovered and tried to crush the robot's arms like he'd done yesterday, but the metal wouldn't budge.

'Trying your same old tricks?' laughed Mrs Sock. 'I've made a few enhancements since our last encounter. I think you'll find it's much stronger now.'

Nelson tried to overpower the robot suit, using every bit of his strength. But it was no use. Even with his super strength, he wasn't strong enough! Nelson started to panic. The robot suit lifted him in the air and started spinning him round and round. All Nelson could see was a blur of books as he struggled to free himself from the robot suit's grip.

'Starting to feel dizzy yet, Mr Invisible?' said Mrs Sock to Nelson.

She started laughing at her own joke when *bop!* Olive knocked Mrs Sock over the head with a beanbag. It didn't hurt her but it did knock her glasses off, which Mrs Sock was using to control the robot suit. Olive stomped on Mrs Sock's glasses with an almighty crunch.

The robot suit instantly lost power, and Nelson fell down on top of it.

'Now's your chance, Nelson!' shouted Olive, running away from a furious Mrs Sock. 'Get that dinosaur hater!'

Nelson scrambled to his feet, but his brain still felt like it was spinning ten times a second. He took a step towards Mrs Sock and fell on his butt. Mrs Sock picked her robot suit up from the floor, pressed a button on the arm and it opened up. She squeezed inside and the suit closed around her.

'Come back here, you,' said a woozy Nelson as he tried to pull himself together.

'Quickly, Nelson, she's getting away!' yelled Olive, hiding in the corner in case Mrs Sock decided to pay her back for the beanbag-to-the-head with a few lasers.

Finally back on his feet, Nelson grabbed Mrs Sock by her metal shoulders. Maybe he could try a headbutt move . . . but he could barely hold himself up. He still felt really unsteady, like he was standing up on a boat in the middle of a storm. His stomach was churning. He felt like he was going to . . .

BLARG!

Nelson threw up all over Mrs Sock's

shiny robot suit, instantly becoming
visible again and losing his super
strength.

'Disgusting!' shouted Mrs Sock.

Nelson collapsed on the floor, unable
to move.

'Some hero you turned out to be!'
said Mrs Sock. She looked over at Olive

cowering in the corner. 'Tell your class I quit teaching forever,' she said with a grin. 'Now that I've dealt with you two, I'm changing careers and moving on to *much* bigger things. You'll never have to worry about excursions to the Dinosaur Museum ever again.'

Mrs Sock walked through the library door, then paused. 'And don't bother trying to call for help with your fancy watches,' she chuckled. 'I disabled them with an electromagnetic pulse the moment I saw you wearing them.' She closed the door and locked it behind her, leaving Olive and a knocked-out Nelson trapped in the library with no escape.

Chapter 13

Unconscious on the library floor, Nelson dreamed that he was at a restaurant about to eat the enormous cheeseburger he'd drawn in art class that afternoon. He was milliseconds away from taking his first delicious bite when he was rudely awakened by Olive shaking him back into consciousness.

'Did you enjoy your nap?' said Olive.

Nelson sat up, his head throbbing. 'What do you think her grand plans are?' he asked.

'Isn't it obvious?' replied Olive. 'Now that she's destroyed all the dinosaur books, she's going to destroy the other place we can learn about dinosaurs: the museum.'

'Not the Dinosaur Museum!' pleaded Nelson. 'That's the only place that sells waffles in the shape of dinosaur bones!'

'This lady really wants every kid to forget that dinosaurs ever existed,' said Olive as her stomach growled loudly. 'I need to get *you* out of here so you can catch her, and I need to get *myself* out of here so I can eat! I'm starving – all I ate today was the salad off your sandwich!'

'That lady is way too powerful,' said a defeated Nelson. 'All the pumpkin in the world wouldn't make me anywhere near as strong as I'd need to be to beat her.'

Olive put her hands on her grumbling tummy. 'Wait a minute . . .' she said, and ran over to her schoolbag. 'We shared your lunch today, Nelson, but we didn't even touch mine!' She pulled out her lunchbox and flipped open the lid. 'Mrs Sock may have seen the book inside my bag,' she said to a puzzled Nelson, 'but she didn't see our secret weapon: baingan bharta!'

Olive held an eggplant-curry-filled spoon towards Nelson.

'Are you sure about this, Olive?' he asked, definitely not sure about this himself.

'Oh, I'm sure, all right,' said Olive. 'What's the one thing the evil robot lady would never expect to fight today?'

Nelson stared blankly at Olive.

'A great, big, powerful, terrifying, ferocious, PURPLE dinosaur!' she said excitedly. 'Let's do this!'

'I don't have a choice, do I?' said Nelson, who began counting down as Olive thrust the spoon towards him.

'Five, four, three . . .'

Olive got impatient and shoved the baingan bharta into Nelson's mouth before he finished counting. Nelson swallowed the mushy eggplant and his whole body began to shake. He felt his muscles tense and his teeth get sharper. He felt his arms tingle, then the rest of his body grew ten times in size while his skin turned purple. A long tail shot out of his butt and slapped the ground beneath him.

Nelson may have felt powerless before, but now he felt like he could take on anyone and anything. The gigantic purple Nelson-saurus rex stood proudly and let out an enormous *ROOOOOOOAR.*

Then the purple dinosaur's best friend climbed up his tail, onto his back and perched between his shoulders.

'Giddy-up, Nelson,' Olive yelled, before letting out a roar that was almost as loud as his.

Chapter 14

Nelson's dad always said that in order to make an omelette, you have to break a few eggs. Today, the omelette was the Dinosaur Museum, and the eggs were the school library's wall.

CRASH!

The gigantic purple Nelson-saurus smashed through the wall of his school library and jumped over the fence as

Olive shouted directions to the Dinosaur Museum.

'Left!' screamed Olive as Nelson accidentally trampled a bus stop.

'Right!' she yelled as Nelson knocked over a stop sign with his tail.

'Jump!' she shouted as Nelson leapt over a taxi.

Nelson gritted his giant teeth and tried to ignore all the drivers staring at him when he jumped over their cars. It was 5 pm and lots of people were on their way home from work. The commuters probably expected traffic, but there's no way they expected a giant purple dinosaur with a girl riding on its back. Nelson was pretty sure nobody would recognise him in his dinosaur form (usually he was much shorter and much less purple), but he tried to move as fast as he could so that nobody would see Olive.

While the traffic was shocking,

Nelson's dinosaur jumping skills meant that he and Olive were making great time. In just thirty seconds, they were halfway from the school to the museum. This would usually take Nelson's mum five to ten minutes to drive. Getting around as a dinosaur was an awesome time saver; it was just a shame about the insane amount of damage he was causing in the street while he ran.

In the next thirty seconds, Nelson broke three windows, crushed two parked cars, knocked over seven street signs, flattened one set of traffic lights and terrified thirty-two dogs. But it was worth it. Together, Olive and the

Nelson-saurus were going to protect the pride and joy of their town: its impressive dinosaur-skeleton collection.

The Greenmore Dinosaur Museum was home to the only complete *Diplodocus* skeleton in the country, as well as a *Triceratops* skeleton, a *Stegosaurus* skeleton and a brand-new pterosaur collection. But Nelson was most excited to see if he was taller than the *T-rex* skeleton in the middle of the museum. He was also most excited to see how many bone-shaped waffles he'd be able to eat at his current size.

Nelson came to a screeching halt just outside the museum. He was worried that he'd have to smash his way inside, but someone had beat them there and blown a huge hole in the side of the museum, just big enough for a dinosaur with a girl on his back to squeeze into.

Chapter 15

When Nelson was invisible, he was quite good at sneaking through secret enemy bases undetected, but right now he was not invisible. He was gigantic, purple and a dinosaur. No amount of shushing from Olive atop his back would stop his enormous body from making way too much noise as they tried to creep into the dark museum without Mrs Sock noticing them.

The museum closed at 5 pm, and it looked like all the staff had left before Mrs Sock had exploded her way inside. Maybe Nelson had jumped over their cars on the way here. He couldn't hear anyone in the museum with them, but he could see a dim light way up ahead.

Nelson tried his hardest to creep slowly through the museum's entrance on his tippy toes, but the sight of a dinosaur on its tippy toes was one of the stupidest things Olive had ever seen, so she was the one who was at risk of blowing their cover as she muffled her laughter.

They had just made it into the lobby when Nelson bashed his head into the men's toilet sign, sending it crashing to

TINKA   TINKA TINKA   TINKA

the ground with a thud. Usually, this would've made Nelson cry out in pain, but his dinosaur head was as hard as a rock.

'What was that?' shouted Mrs Sock's voice from inside the herbivore exhibition. 'Who's there?'

'It's the police!' yelled Olive, unconvincingly. 'We have the place surrounded. Come out with your hands up.'

Mrs Sock laughed. 'I thought I told you kids, the Dinosaur Museum excursion is cancelled!' she shouted. 'Now, why don't you run along home before I call your parents.'

'We know what you're here to do,' said Olive, looking through the darkness for Mrs Sock. 'And we're not going to let you do it!'

'Oh really?' said the robot lady, stepping into the light. 'And who's strong enough to stop me?'

'He is!' shouted Olive. 'Tell her how strong you are, Nelson!'

Nelson let out a roar so loud, the ground shook like an earthquake had hit. Nelson couldn't see Mrs Sock's face beneath her robot suit, but he was certain she was terrified.

'A d-d-d-dinosaur?' she stuttered in disbelief, no longer the tough-as-nails

teacher who gave Nelson detention
and beat him up earlier.
Mrs Sock was staring at
her greatest fear, and
she was terrified.

Nelson took a step
towards her with a
big toothy grin. Olive slid

down his tail and climbed on top of a *Triceratops* skeleton.

'Stay back!' screamed the spooked Mrs Sock, before aiming her lasers at Nelson. 'I was going to blow up the *Stegosaurus* skeleton first, but I guess I have to change my plans.'

Mrs Sock flew into the air and flipped over Nelson, firing lasers at him. But Nelson's purple dinosaur skin was too tough for the lasers to penetrate, although they did make him extra angry. He stomped his feet and blew hot air out of his nostrils.

'It's time to show her who's more powerful, Nelson,' said Olive. 'A robot . . . or a dinosaur!'

'I think you mean ro*bots*,' said Mrs Sock, tapping a button on the side of her glove as she turned away from Nelson. 'I've just invited a few friends.'

Chapter 16

Nelson heard what sounded like twenty aeroplanes flying towards the museum, and saw blinking lights approaching through the windows. Nelson wondered what was headed their way.

'It's been nice knowing you,' said Mrs Sock, rising into the air. 'But dinosaurs should stay extinct.'

Crash! The museum windows shattered, sending glass flying everywhere. Nelson suddenly found himself surrounded by twenty empty robot suits.

'These prototypes might not be as strong as I am now, but they should be more than enough to send you back to the Ice Age, where you belong!' Mrs Sock laughed as she flew deeper into the museum.

Olive jumped from the *Triceratops*

134

skeleton onto
Nelson's back.

She pulled a ruler out of her
schoolbag and held it above her
head like a mighty sword.
She pointed the ruler at
one of the robot suits.
'On your marks,' she
shouted into Nelson's
ear. 'Get set . . .
CHAAARGE!'

Nelson roared and
stomped towards
the closest robot,
pulling it out of the
air with his mouth

135

and crushing it to pieces with his sharp teeth. Eating a robot was significantly easier than eating an eggplant.

'Nelson, on your left!' shouted Olive as Nelson smashed a robot against the wall.

'Right!' she yelled as Nelson flicked his tail at a robot and sent it crashing into the museum's information desk.

'Jump!' she screamed as Nelson soared through the air and landed on two unsuspecting robots, flattening them like metal pancakes. Nelson wondered if he'd be allowed to sign up for karate classes in his dinosaur form once all of this was over.

STOMP!

Nelson kicked, bit, stamped, stomped, punched, crunched, bashed and smashed his way through all of the robots. Robots were *much* tastier than vegetables, and now there was just one left.

'Self-destruct sequence initiated,' said the robot. 'Detonation in five, four, three . . .'

'Nelson, do something!' screamed Olive.

Nelson knew exactly what to do at the end of a countdown. He bent down to the robot, opened his mouth wide and swallowed the robot whole.

There was a muffled *boom* from deep within Nelson's dinosaur stomach, and when he opened his mouth again, smoke came out. Other than that, Nelson was fine.

He'd saved Olive – and the museum – from being blown up, and now he needed to save a bunch of skeletons too.

Chapter 17

Nelson and Olive crept through the museum, looking for Mrs Sock.

'I think I prefer you as a dinosaur, Nelson,' said Olive, patting Nelson on the back. 'You complain a lot less.'

Nelson growled. Not because of Olive's joke, but because he could see Mrs Sock crouched beneath the *Tyrannosaurus rex* skeleton, placing a device at its feet.

Nelson sprinted towards her, his stomps making the entire museum shake.

Mrs Sock fired as many lasers at him as she could, but nothing slowed him down. He headbutted Mrs Sock with his big dinosaur skull and sent her flying. Mrs Sock's rocket boots kicked in while she was midair, and she flew back into Nelson, knocking him over.

Olive held on to Nelson as he got back on his feet and chased after Mrs Sock, but she had flown just high enough to be out of his reach.

'You're too late anyway!' said Mrs Sock, hovering above Nelson. 'I've planted enough bombs to demolish the entire museum with the dinosaurs still in it – including you!'

Nelson launched himself towards her with all of his dino-might. Mrs Sock tried to move further from his reach, but he managed to grab onto her foot with his teeth.

'Let go of me!' yelled Mrs Sock, but it was time for some payback. Nelson spun round and round, spinning Mrs Sock around the room like a ragdoll. Then he flicked Mrs Sock into the air, opened his mouth wide and waited for her to fall inside. *Chomp!* He trapped the evil robot lady in his mouth.

'You're not going to eat her, are you,

Nelson?' asked Olive. 'I don't think you'd get any good superpowers from doing that.'

Nelson shook his head, but then jolted upright. Mrs Sock was punching him from the inside of his mouth! Nelson fought to keep his mouth closed, but Mrs Sock was pushing his jaws open, bit by bit. Her suit was as strong as a dinosaur!

Soon, Mrs Sock had pried Nelson's mouth completely open. He tried to swat her away with his tiny arms, but he couldn't reach. Mrs Sock blasted out of his mouth and up to the ceiling, then shot back down to Nelson and swatted

him on the snout, knocking him flat on the floor.

'Get up, Nelson!' begged Olive, as Mrs Sock put both arms together and charged a hyper beam from her hands. Nelson jumped to his left just as Mrs Sock fired the bright blue laser beam past his head, narrowly missing the *Stegosaurus* skeleton behind him.

Mrs Sock was charging up again when Nelson knocked her over with his tail, sending sparks flying. She rocketed back at Nelson, headbutting him with her shiny metal helmet at full speed and sending herself, Nelson and Olive crashing into an exhibit of exotic birds that a museum staff member once told them were descendants of dinosaurs.

Nelson and Mrs Sock slowly picked themselves back up again. Nelson could barely stand. His purple skin was bruised and burned, and his breathing was slow. All he wanted to do was curl up and go to sleep for a while.

Mrs Sock wasn't looking too hot either. Her suit was a mangled mess of exposed wires that were sparking and smouldering. Her helmet had a crack in it, and one of her rocket boots wasn't working at all.

'You've left me with no choice,' said Mrs Sock, lifting a remote in her hand.

'I'll just have to blow up the museum with us inside it. My suit should protect me, but you two meddlers won't be so lucky!'

Nelson looked around for Olive so he could protect her, but she was searching through the bird exhibit for something. What was she doing?

Mrs Sock lifted her finger towards the remote. Olive pulled a large feather from a stuffed peacock in the exhibit and waved it above her head.

'Any last words before I push the button?' asked Mrs Sock.

Nelson had one last thing to say. He opened his mouth as wide as possible and let out the biggest roar he'd ever roared. While he was roaring, Olive ran up his tail, climbed onto his back and swung round his neck, shoving the peacock feather into his mouth and tickling his tonsils.

Nelson aimed his mouth at Mrs Sock and vomited enough dino-spew on her to fill a swimming pool, knocking the remote from her hand. As Nelson returned to his usual size and colour, Mrs Sock's now-soaking-wet robot suit short-circuited and crackled.

Olive grabbed the remote and stood over Mrs Sock, who was trapped inside her broken robot suit.

'Robots might be as powerful as dinosaurs,' said Olive to Mrs Sock, 'but nothing is stronger than Nelson's vomit!'

Chapter 18

Suddenly, all the lights in the museum turned on and the sound of voices could be heard echoing through the halls.

'What now?' said Nelson, wiping his lips. He wondered if it was museum security heading their way. How were they going to explain this?

'We better hide!' said Olive.

But half the museum had been smashed. There was barely anything left to hide under.

'Agents Hunter and Sadana, is that you?' asked a familiar voice.

Nelson and Olive stepped out of the shadows to see that it was Agent Cherry! She'd arrived with a handful of secret agents, all dressed in bright-red suits.

'I got reports that a gigantic purple dinosaur was causing havoc in the city. Don't tell me that was you guys,' she said.

Nelson and Olive laughed nervously.

Agent Cherry lifted her hat as she observed the mess in front of her.

'What on earth happened here?' she said, carefully stepping over a pool of purple vomit.

Olive tossed Agent Cherry the remote, walked over to the collapsed Mrs Sock and pulled off her helmet. 'This is your book thief, Agent Cherry,' said Olive. 'She's also a robotics expert, an explosives enthusiast, a dinosaur hater and a *terrible* relief teacher.'

'She told us her name was Mrs Sock,' said Nelson. 'But that's a fake name if ever I've heard one!'

'Actually, that is her real name,' said Agent Cherry. 'Full name: *Toni* Sock. One of the best robotic engineers in the country. But instead of using her inventions to help people, she used them to travel the world and destroy anything she could find about dinosaurs.'

'Don't you dare say the d-word in my presence!' shouted Mrs Sock as Agent Cherry lifted her up and put her in handcuffs.

'Are you going to take her to jail?' asked Olive.

'Are you kidding me?' said Agent Cherry. 'We could absolutely use a robotics expert like her at S.Q.U.A.S.H.'

Nelson and Olive looked at Agent Cherry in shock. S.Q.U.A.S.H. stood for *Secret Quiet Union of Aspiring Super Heroes*, and Agent Cherry was considering recruiting Nelson. Nelson didn't realise it was a secret quiet union of PROVEN SUPER VILLAINS as well though! What could Agent Cherry possibly want from Mrs Sock?

'Who knows?' continued Agent

Cherry. 'Maybe I can get her to make robot suits for you two.'

'I'd sooner never build a robot again than build one for these despicable interlopers!' spat Mrs Sock. 'My beautiful robots will *never* assist dinosaur lovers.'

'We'll see about that,' said Agent Cherry to Mrs Sock, before she walked over to Nelson and Olive. 'You guys did great today,' she told them. 'Olive, you helped take down an A-ranked villain, and you did it without superpowers. Your quick wits and calm decisiveness continue to impress me.'

Olive smiled, a little embarrassed, as Agent Cherry turned to Nelson.

'And as for you,' she said, pointing her finger directly between Nelson's eyes. 'First you were super strong, then you were invisible and today you're a dinosaur? You adapt to your new powers so quickly! How do you do it?'

Nelson looked at Agent Cherry and said with a smile, 'Whenever I'm in a tough situation, I just ask myself: what would the strongest, toughest and biggest old dinosaur I know do?'

'The biggest old dinosaur you know?' asked Agent Cherry. 'Who on earth is that?'

Suddenly, a very cross voice blared from Nelson's watch. 'He's talking about me! How dare you call your grandma an old dinosaur!'

IF NELSON'S GRANDMA WAS A DINOSAUR

Olive started cracking up, and Nelson covered his mouth with shock. His grandma's face stared up at him from his watch.

'Do you know how many times I've tried calling you two today?' said Nelson's grandma. 'At least a hundred! And neither of you answered. I was about to come to the city to find you myself!'

'We're sorry!' said Nelson and Olive in unison.

'Mrs Sock disabled our watches, and they've only just come back online now,' Nelson explained.

Nelson's watch suddenly lit up with two-hundred messages. They were all from his grandma.

'Who is Mrs Sock?' asked Nelson's confused grandma, trying her best to figure out what was going on. 'And why are you surrounded by dinosaur skeletons?'

'I promise I'll call you back later,' said Nelson. 'We've got everything under control – but wait till you hear what happens to me when I eat an eggplant!'

Nelson ended the call before his grandma could ask a million more questions.

A team of secret agents gathered around Mrs Sock and started to drag her out of the museum.

'You can't imprison me for long!' screamed Mrs Sock as she was halfway out the door. 'As soon as I get out, I'm going to erase all dinosaurs from existence, once and for all, starting with you, Nelson Hunter!'

Nelson was speechless. Luckily, his best friend wasn't.

'Bring it on, you tin can!' shouted Olive as she put her arm around

Nelson. 'Dinosaurs are WAY cooler than robots!'

'And one more thing,' shouted Nelson, joining in. 'You were the *worst* teacher *ever*!'

Nelson and Olive laughed as Agent Cherry took a look around at the museum. Glass and debris were scattered all over the exhibits.

'We should probably get you kids home so my team can clean this place up,' said Agent Cherry.

Nelson suddenly sprinted in the opposite direction of the exit.

'Nelson, where are you going?' asked Olive as Nelson jumped over a fallen

pot plant and slid over to a food stall
that had been blasted to pieces.

'Yes! They're still warm,' said Nelson,
happily. He rustled through a box
of food products, then raised his
hands above his head. In each, he
held one of the museum's signature

bone-shaped waffles. He'd eaten nothing but vegetables all day. It was time for some real food.

'Does anyone want any?' asked Nelson, his mouth full of waffles.

Olive and Agent Cherry looked at Nelson in disbelief as he swallowed waffle after waffle, barely breathing in between bites.

Sure, he could become super strong, go invisible and turn into a dinosaur, but his real superpower was clearly eating junk food.

About the Author

Andrew Levins has been a DJ since he was a teenager, and a food writer for almost as long. He cut his teeth as one of the inaugural DJs on FBi radio, plays most major Australian music festivals and hosts the longest-running hip-hop night in Sydney. His articles have been published by the *Sydney Morning Herald*, ABC Life, VICE, SBS, *Good Food Guide* and *Time Out*. In 2007 he co-founded the youth music charity Heaps Decent (with Diplo and Nina Las Vegas), and in 2009 he was named one of Sydney's 100 Most Influential People by the *Sydney Morning Herald*. Since then he's had two kids, run a successful restaurant, released a cookbook and started no fewer than five podcasts. The Nelson series are his first books for children.

About the Illustrator

Katie Kear is a young British illustrator and has been creating artwork for as long as she can remember. She loves creating new worlds and characters, and hopes to spread joy and happiness with her illustrations.

As a child, her favourite memories always involved reading. Whether it was reading her first picture books with her mother before bed, and imagining new stories for the characters, or as an older child reading chapter books into the night, she remembers always having a love for books! This is what made her pursue her career in illustration.

In her spare time she loves drawing, adventures in nature, chocolate, stationery, the smell of cherries and finding new inspirational artists!

Olive's Favourite Baingan Bharta

Ingredients

2 medium eggplants

½ a lime

2 tablespoons of ghee or vegetable oil

1 red onion, peeled and chopped

1 teaspoon of cumin seeds

4 cloves of garlic, peeled and finely chopped

1 inch of fresh ginger, peeled and grated

2 tomatoes, chopped

1 green chilli (optional)

1 teaspoon of fresh turmeric, grated, or ½ a teaspoon
    of turmeric powder

1 teaspoon of salt

½ a bunch of coriander, finely chopped

2 teaspoons of garam masala

Method

1. Preheat oven to 220°C (428°F). Alternatively, light the grill or broiler to its highest heat.

2. Wash the eggplants, then use a fork to prick them all over their skins. Line a baking tray with foil, and put both eggplants on the tray. Roast the eggplants in the oven or under the grill, turning every few minutes, until their skins have started to burn and blister all over. When they start to collapse and are soft inside, they're ready. (You can test their softness with a fork. It'll take about 20 minutes under the grill or around 30 minutes in the oven.) Allow the roasted eggplants to cool.

3. When the roasted eggplants are cool enough to handle, cut their tops off, peel back some of their skin and scoop the flesh into a bowl. Mash the flesh with a fork, and squeeze the lime juice over the top. Give the mixture a stir and put to one side.

4. Heat the ghee or oil in a pot over a medium heat. When it starts to shimmer, add the chopped onion and cumin seeds. Stir for five minutes, until the onions start to brown.

5. Add the garlic, ginger, tomatoes, chilli (if using), turmeric and salt to the pot, and cook for ten minutes, stirring occasionally to stop the mixture from sticking to the bottom of the pot.

6. Stir in the mashed eggplant and cook for a further five minutes. Remove from the heat, then stir in the coriander and garam masala. Serve with basmati rice.

HAVE YOU READ?

Baxter
The Bear Dog

Lee Stewart Gilmore

FOR EVERY CAVACHON OWNER WHEN
SOMEONE SAYS......WHAT BREED IS THAT?
HERE IS YOUR ANSWER....

Baxter

Lee Stewart Gilmore

Other Titles by the Author

The Leadhills Mining Bear Company
Book 1 – A Most Unusual Day
Book 2 – Hillbillies and Jam
Book 3 – Mr Symington's Steamboat
Book 4 – Santa's Stopover

Reuben – The Little Stowaway Reindeer

Cavalier Capers
Chester Don't-Touch and The Flower Garden

For Adults
Courage and Clowns (Also on Kindle)

BAXTER THE BEAR DOG

Baxter was a happy little dog. He lived with his Mummy and two brothers in a little village up in the hills. Each day was a new adventure for Baxter. He had lots of exciting things to do. Some days he played in the garden with his brothers. Even on a rainy day Baxter was just as happy to be inside playing with his toys.

And if he was very good he got to help his Mummy in her little Teddy Bear Shop. He loved meeting all the people who came in and they all made a fuss of him and told him how cute he was. He liked that.

His favourite thing of all was going for a run up in the hills. He chased his brothers and ran through the heather. It was the best time ever. Sometimes they met neighbours up on the hill with their dogs. Baxter thought he was the luckiest dog in the world.

"Come on Fallon," shouted Baxter. "I'll race you to the top."

Very soon the two little dogs were scrambling up the hillside. They fell over each other and tumbled about in the heather. Their older brother thought their games were a bit silly so he preferred to walk beside mummy.

On their way home from their run they met a woman they hadn't seen before. Baxter was very unsure of people he didn't know so he hid behind Mummy.

"What beautiful Cavaliers," she said, looking at Baxter's brothers. "Aren't they just adorable?"
Then she looked at Baxter and said,
"What on earth is this?"
"He's a Cavachon," said Baxter's Mummy.
"Oh he's not a real breed then? He's a funny little thing," she said as she walked away.

Baxter was very upset as they walked home. He didn't want people thinking he looked funny.

"Why did that lady say I wasn't real?" he asked his brother.

"I don't know," said Fallon. "But humans are very odd at times and that's why you don't go near people that you don't know. Sometimes they say really strange things. You just learn to ignore them."

"But I want to be a real dog and I don't want people looking at me and saying I look funny," said Baxter. He was very sad.

Baxter spent the rest of the morning in his bed, just

feeling sad. His brothers tried to get him to play but he didn't want to go into the garden. He wanted to know how to become a real dog.

His brother Fallon tried to cheer him up. "You are a real dog Baxter. Mummy chose you specially to be our brother and she wouldn't have picked you if you hadn't been a real dog. So stop being silly and come out and play."

"I don't want to play," said Baxter. "I'm just going to lie here and feel sad." He curled up in his bed and closed his eyes. Maybe a little sleep would help.

When Baxter woke up from his sleep he realised what he had to do. He had lots of friends and he decided to ask them about being a real dog. He knew they wouldn't lie to him and whatever they said, he would believe because they were his friends.

First of all he asked Mummy.

"Baxter I'm really busy at the moment," said Mummy. "Could you run along and play for a little while."

"It's okay," said Baxter. "I have lots of other people to talk to today so I'll go speak to them first."

The first person Baxter went to speak to was the bird. He jumped up on the sofa.

"Excuse me Mr Budgie, can I ask you a question please?" asked Baxter.

"Please stop there, that's close enough if you don't mind," said the bird. "And I'm not a budgie I'm a cockatiel. A cockatiel is an entirely different thing."

"I'm sorry," said Baxter. "I didn't know that, but can I ask you something?"

"Yes you can, but could you please stop bouncing around. You do tend to bounce a lot and I don't want you tipping my cage," said the cockatiel.

"I didn't know I bounced," said Baxter.

"Yes you do, all the time, bounce, bounce, bounce. Now what did you want to ask me?"

"How do I become a real dog?" said Baxter.

"I'm not sure what you mean, you are already a dog. How much more of a dog do you want to be?" asked the cockatiel.

"But am I real?" said Baxter.

The cockatiel thought for a moment. "I'm not sure I'm following this conversation," he said. "Let me see…. you bark like a dog, you sleep in a dog bed, and you have two brothers and they are both dogs. I'd say you were definitely a dog. Now does that answer your question?"

"I am not sure, I'll have to go and think about it," said Baxter. "But thank you so much Mr Cockatiel, it was very nice talking to you. And I promise I won't bounce near your cage again."

"Thank you little dog, that would be very much appreciated," said the cockatiel as he tucked his head under his wing and went back to sleep.

Baxter wasn't sure that he really had an answer to his question so his next visit was to the Bear Shop. He thought maybe the bears had the answer.

He very quietly opened the door. He wasn't meant to be in the shop on his own. Mummy wouldn't like it at all.

"Hello," he said very quietly. "Can I come in?"

"Who said that?" said Mr Cameron the bear on the top shelf. "Someone said 'Hello'."

"It was me," said Baxter. "I want to ask you something?"

"It's the little Bear Dog, yes, yes, come in," said Mr Taylor the bear who wore spectacles. "What can we do for you little one?"

"Well, when I was out for my walk today we met a lady who said I wasn't a real dog and I want to be a real dog. What can I do about it?" Baxter looked sad again.

"Now why would anyone say such a thing," said Mr Taylor. "Of course you're a real dog. What else could you possibly be?"

"She said my brothers were beautiful and all she said about me was that I wasn't real and that I looked funny. Why don't I look more like my brothers?" asked Baxter.

"I don't know the answer to that. We all like you, we call you the Bear Dog," said Mr Taylor.

"Why do you call me that?" asked Baxter

"Actually, I don't know the answer to that either. I think it was Grampa Sam who said it first. Grampa Sam knows everything," said Mr Taylor.

"Maybe I should speak to him?" Baxter looked around but Grampa Sam wasn't in the shop.

"He's sitting outside today in his basket chair. You'll need to wait until Mummy brings him back in and that won't be very long now. So until then perhaps we could try and work out what this real dog business is all about," said Mr Cameron.

The bears all thought very hard. What makes a dog, a real dog.

"Dogs have floppy ears," said Mr Taylor.

"I have floppy ears too," cried Baxter, jumping up and down.

"That's a good start," said Mr Cameron. "Next, dogs have long tails."

Baxter thought for a few minutes. "I don't have a long tail, but I have a very bushy one, does that count?"

"Oh yes I think that ticks off number 2 on the list," laughed Mr Taylor. "It really is a remarkable tail."

"Dogs have large paws," said Mr Cameron

"I have large paws," squealed Baxter. "That's number 3."

"Dog's have very glossy coats, that's number 4," said Mr Cameron.

Baxter looked down at his thick coat. "I don't think my coat is very shiny, but it's thick and has lots of curls."

"That sounds about right. You have a wet nose and big eyes and I think that about covers everything. I declare you a real dog," said Mr Taylor.

"Then why did that lady say I wasn't real?" said Baxter, looking sad again.

"Well I don't understand that at all. We can all see you and you look very much like a dog," said Mr Cameron.

At exactly that moment Mummy brought Grampa Sam back inside.

"What are you doing in here Baxter?" she said. "Please don't touch anything," and off she went back through to the house.

Baxter explained his problem to Grampa Sam. He was the biggest bear in the shop and he was very clever.

"Well now little one," said Grampa Sam. "That's a very serious problem, but one that I know I can answer."

"I knew you would know," said Baxter

"Do you remember what I told you about when a bear leaves the shop, and you were so sad because you wouldn't see them again."

"Yes, I remember," said Baxter. "Children love a teddy bear more than anything in the world, and when they choose one they love it for their whole life."

Grampa Sam was very pleased that he hadn't forgotten

"Well unfortunately it's not always the same for little puppies. Sometimes people choose one and then they decide they don't want it and some of them spend a long time finding someone to love them."

"That's sad," said Baxter.

"It is very sad but then someone had a bright idea," said Grampa Sam. "They made a Cavachon. A little dog that was so special, everyone would love them."

"That's me," said Baxter happily. "I'm special."

"Not just special, but special in three different ways," said Grampa Sam. "Firstly they took a

Cavalier, just like your brothers, because they were kind and gentle. Then they added a big chunk of Bichon. That's where you get your beautiful coat. It's so thick and curly, people just want to cuddle it. And lastly and possibly the most special of all, they sprinkled you with magic dust and made you look like a teddy bear."

"Is that why you call me Bear Dog?" asked Baxter.

Grampa Sam laughed. "Yes, you are the only dog in the world filled with the magic of a teddy bear. And that means when someone chooses a Cavachon, they have a little dog they will love for their whole life. So you see Baxter, someone went to a lot of trouble to make you."

"Wow, I never knew that," said Baxter. "I am a real dog and if I didn't know then lots of people don't know yet either, so I have to tell them. Thank you Grampa Sam."

"You see Baxter, sometimes it's so much better to be different."

Baxter was back to being his happy little self.

"Now you better run along before Mummy comes looking for you. Goodnight little Bear Dog."

"Goodnight Grampa Sam, goodnight bears," said Baxter.

"Goodnight little Bear Dog," said all the bears.

Baxter ran back through to the house to find his brothers. He couldn't wait to tell them.

In the Bear Shop the bears were all congratulating Grampa Sam on doing such a good job.

"Oh there's a little bit of magic in all of us," said Grampa Sam. "You just need to use your imagination. Our little Bear Dog has a very special place in this world, he just hadn't realised it. Now when someone asks him what he is, he can explain it."

Baxter had been very excited all evening and now it was bedtime and he was finding it hard to sleep.

"Baxter could you please put out the light?" said his brothers. "We are trying to sleep."

"I'm too happy to sleep," said Baxter.

"I don't think it's possible to be too happy to sleep, just try it," said a sleepy Fallon.

"Maybe it's all the magic in me. Grampa Sam says that's what makes me different," said Baxter.

"Oh you're different all right," said Fallon. "There's no doubt about that !"

24287264R00018

Printed in Great Britain
by Amazon